Climb Your Inner Mountain

You are Reaching the Peak of YOUR Potential

Author

Sandy S

Copyright © <2024> <Sandy S.>

All Rights Reserved.

This book has been self-published with all reasonable efforts taken to make the material error-free by the author. No part of this book shall be used, or reproduced in any manner whatsoever without written permission from the author, except in the case of brief quotations embodied in critical articles and reviews.

The Author of this book is solely responsible and liable for its content including but not limited to the views, representations, descriptions, statements, information, opinions and references ["Content"]. The Content of this book shall not constitute or be construed or deemed to reflect the opinion or expression of the Publisher or Editor. Neither the Publisher nor Editor endorse or approve the Content of this book or guarantee the reliability, accuracy or completeness of the Content published herein and do not make any representations or warranties of any kind, express or implied, including but not limited to the implied warranties of merchantability, fitness for a particular purpose. The Publisher and Editor shall not be liable whatsoever for any errors, omissions, whether such errors or omissions result from negligence, accident, or any other cause or claims for loss or damages of any kind, including without limitation, indirect or consequential loss or damage arising out of use, inability to use, or about the reliability, accuracy or sufficiency of the information contained in this book.

Made with ♥ on the Notion Press Platform

www.notionpress.com

To every woman who has ever doubted her strength,
to every soul who has climbed through pain and emerged stronger,
*and to the one woman who has always believed in me—**myself**.*

This book is for you. For the ones still climbing, for the ones who have already reached the peak, and for those who are discovering their power, one step at a time. May you always remember that your mountain is yours to climb—and you are more than capable of reaching the top.

With love and gratitude,

Sandy S

Contents

Foreword

In every woman's life, there comes a moment—sometimes quiet, sometimes loud—when the call to rise above the noise of doubt and fear becomes undeniable. It's the moment when we realize that the only way to move forward, to truly live, is to embrace the mountain of our own potential. This book, *Climb Your Own Mountain*, is not just a guide, but a companion on that very journey.

Each of us carries within us a mountain—one that's uniquely ours, formed by our experiences, dreams, and challenges. And yet, too often, we find ourselves standing at the base, unsure of how to take the first step. We may hesitate, questioning whether we are strong enough to climb, or whether the summit is within our reach. This book reminds you that **you are already equipped** with everything you need to ascend.

Through its pages, you'll find not only the inspiration to rise but also the practical tools to build your strength—mentally, emotionally, and spiritually. This is a journey of self-discovery, one that will teach you how to conquer your doubts, embrace your inner power, and celebrate the woman you were always meant to be.

As you embark on this life-changing adventure, know that you are never alone. You are part of a sisterhood of women who have faced their own mountains and emerged stronger. *Climb Your Own Mountain* invites you to do the same—no matter how steep or rocky the path may seem.

Get ready to challenge your limits, push through your fears, and experience the thrill of scaling new heights. This book is a reminder that the greatest journey you will ever take is the one that leads you to yourself.

So, take a deep breath, steady your heart, and start your climb. The view from the top is worth every step.

Preface

Do you ever feel like life is a never-ending climb?
Yes it is!
Life is filled with mountains of expectations, social pressures, and the shadows of self-doubt that can loom over our dreams. We all face these struggles—whether they are universal challenges or our own inner battles. It can often feel overwhelming, like we're constantly scaling a steep peak, unsure of how to reach the top.

But here's the thing: the climb is worth it.

Like you, I've experienced my own struggles, and I've witnessed the struggles of others—especially the struggles women face in their personal journeys of growth and self-discovery. This book is not just about a woman named Tara—though she is the story's protagonist. This is your story. It is about your climb, your battles, the fears that whisper doubts in your ear, and the incredible strength you possess to rise above them.

In these pages, you'll join Tara on her inspiring journey as she navigates through the challenges of life, discovering her inner strength and resilience along the way. But what you will find in Tara's journey is not just a fictional story—it is a reflection of your own. It mirrors the universal struggles and inner turmoil that we all face at different points in our lives.

This book is your personal climbing guide, filled with empowering stories, practical tools, and relatable experiences designed to help you embrace your own journey of self-discovery.

It is my hope that as you read, you'll find the courage to confront your own mountains and discover the inner strength that will propel you to the peaks of your potential.

As you embark on this journey, remember: this climb is yours alone. Take it at your own pace. Celebrate every small victory. And know that with every challenge, you are growing, evolving, and rising above. You are capable of greatness, and I am honoured to be a part of your journey as you Climb Your Inner Peaks.

With warmth and encouragement,

Sandy S.

Acknowledgments

Writing *Climb Your Own Mountain* has been an incredible journey, and it's only fitting that I take a moment to acknowledge the people who have walked with me, encouraged me, and helped shape this work.

First and foremost, I want to thank the women in my life—those who have shown me what true strength, resilience, and self-discovery look like. You are the inspiration for every word on these pages. Whether you've been my friend, my mentor, or my colleague, you've demonstrated time and time again that every mountain is climbable when we have the courage to face it. Your stories have been the fuel for my own journey, and for that, I am forever grateful.

To my family and friends—thank you for your unwavering support. Your belief in me, even during moments when I doubted myself, has been a constant source of strength.

This book would not have been possible without the support, strength, and challenges I've encountered along the way.

To those who weren't there, thank you as well. Though your absence and challenges sometimes made the path harder, they taught me to fight on my own, to stand firm in my truth, and to find strength within myself. In the end, your absence became my greatest teacher, inspiring me to rise above and persevere, knowing that the journey is mine to conquer.

To every moment of pain, stress, and hardship I've faced—thank you. You have all been my silent mentors, each experience adding another layer of resilience, and each struggle sparking the inspiration to write this book. Through the challenges, I found the courage to discover my true self, and now, I hope these words serve as a guide for other women who may be facing their own mountains.

Finally, I want to thank every woman who has shared her story with me, whether in person or through the pages of history. Your strength, courage, and perseverance have shaped my own, and it is because of you that I am able to share this journey with others.

May this book help you find your own strength, climb your own mountain, and know that you are never alone.

With heartfelt thanks and love,

Sandy

Prologue

There is a mountain within each of us.

It is not a mountain made of stone or rock, but one that rises from the very core of who we are. It is shaped by our experiences, our dreams, our challenges, and, most importantly, by the way we see ourselves. For many, this mountain remains hidden, shrouded by self-doubt, fear, and the weight of the world's expectations. But for those who dare to climb, this mountain becomes the path to the truest version of themselves.

Climb Your Own Mountain is an ***invitation*** to you—an invitation to embark on a journey of self-discovery, to awaken the strength within you that you may not even know exists. This book is not about following someone else's path or living up to someone else's standards. It is about uncovering your own potential and stepping into the power that has always been yours.

In these pages, you will find the tools, stories, and insights to help you face your inner mountain. You will be encouraged to confront the fears and doubts that have kept you standing at the base, unsure of how to begin the climb. You will be reminded that every summit, no matter how high, is reached one step at a time—and that each step brings you closer to the woman you were always meant to be.

But be warned: the climb is not always easy. There will be moments when the summit seems out of reach, when the weight of the journey feels too heavy, and when you wonder if you have the strength to continue. It is in these moments that you will discover the true power of resilience, self-belief, and persistence.

The world will try to tell you who you are, but only you can define yourself. The voices of doubt and insecurity may try to pull you back, but in your heart, you know that the summit is not just a destination—it is a transformation. The woman you become on the journey up that mountain will be stronger, braver, and more alive than the one who started the climb.

I wrote this book to help you navigate that climb. It is a guide for women who are ready to rise above their limitations, to embrace their true selves, and to walk in the fullness of their potential. Whether you are just beginning your climb, or are already halfway up, know this: you are capable of far more than you think.

The summit is waiting. Your journey begins now.

Chapter1.

The Purpose

Recognizing Your Inner Mountain

Men and Women are not Equal?

No...Definitely not.

Men aren't from Mars. Women aren't from Venus.

They're the same species from the same planet but the sexes certainly aren't the same.

Yes, men and women do have biological differences. So, if someone says females are better at giving birth or looking after and nurturing children, I'd say...'Ofcourse!'.

They are more 'intuitive' at understanding what a crying baby wants. Unlike most men, women can hear the baby's cries even in their sleep! That has a biological basis indeed. Male's history has often involved hunting and providing for the family leading to a higher likelihood of developing skills in problem-solving and physical tasks.. So if someone says males are generally better at lifting things or fighting, I'd agree to that too. Because again, this has a biological basis. Majority of men are more muscular and stronger (only physically) - making them better *suited* for physical & hectic jobs, even today. Women are more powerful emotionally. Women have far higher pain thresholds than men! But when someone says females are generally better cooks, or better at house chores, it's only because the gender role they have been assigned. No doubt these roles vary across cultures and time. But E*volution* - has made each of us - male or female - ***more suited*** for a particular kind of job. Note - I said - ***more suited.*** (I am not being stereotyped here.)

Well, there are a lot more differences.

Men typically have thicker skin and not to forget they have larger voice boxes too! Women have better senses of smell and taste. A woman has a larger stomach, kidneys, liver, and appendix than a guy, but she has smaller lungs, thus giving her less breathing capacity than a man.

Wom**en tend to initiate break-ups and divorce more than men. M**ost of the women (Girls) seem to be faithful to attending class, completing assignments, and pursuing excellence in their studies.

A man has five items in his bathroom—a razor, shaving cream, a bar of soap, a toothbrush, and a towel (exception). On the contrary ….'They' say…. The average number of items in a typical women's bathroom is reported to be as high as 437!

Not all but many will agree…..if a woman is driving in unfamiliar surroundings, she will pull out her smartphone for guidance or ask somebody for directions. Men, of course, consider this to be a sign of weakness. They never admit they're lost or ask for directions.

Men are more likely to be colourblind (at least I have heard that). **Men are more likely to be addicted to their smartphones.** Unlike men, Women typically carry their body fat in their hips and thighs. Women typically have lower blood pressure??(I'm not sure though). I have also heard this statement, 'A woman worries about the future until she gets a husband, while a man never worries about the future until he gets a wife'. (Universal Truth, isn't it?)

Apart from all above, 'Research' has found that men fool themselves into thinking someone is romantically interested in them when they aren't. Researchers also discovered that men were much less interested in wearing a condom while having sex.

A British study found that an average man looks in the mirror 23 times per day, while women do it only 16 times per day. Is it? (I'm not sure though). But this has become universal law....When a woman says she will be ready in five minutes, no one can count!

Another thing....no one will believe but as per research, ***Gossip Is NOT Just a Female Thing!***

Communication amongst women has been stigmatized as gossip When boys do it, it's just considered "talking". The term “gossip” dates back to the 12th Century, where the late Old English derived the word “godsibb” ‘god’mother, ‘god’father + a sibling. However, the meaning of gossip gradually changed because of the way society viewed it throughout the years. It started referring to someone you could tell anything.

Gossiping is a behaviour that can be exhibited by both men and women, and it is not inherently linked to gender. It was found to be therapeutic to women who were asked to stay home all day.

Disclaimer: Don’t give me credit for this list, though. There are hundreds of these so-called “differences” floating around all over the internet with absolutely no indications of their sources

"Ladies first"

Isn't it an old-fashioned way of showing respect and affection for women..... just by opening the door and letting them walk in first?

In recent years an increasing number of women believe that allowing a man to open the door for her devalues her in some way – that it makes the man look superior. Why women are portrayed as pure and warm yet helpless and incompetent beings who require cherished protection from men? No need.

But... if that *'gentleman'* is opening a door for a *lady*, this gesture can be as a gift... Ladies can the gift with respect and kindness if it is opened for you!

'Ladies first' is what you say when you want the lady/ladies to go ahead of you, whether it's in a doorway, standing in line, water fountain, go before them in the lift,, in the checkout line, or in some of the restaurant's women are served before the men at the table. etc. It shows that you have manners and consideration for others. In that "golden age" of good manners, "gentlemen" were brought up to treat "ladies" with courtesy. If people had to queue for a buffet at a private social event, the instruction would be given, "Ladies first!" We can take it to an extreme with the "women and children first" in emergencies. (Let's not forget Titanic!)

Sometimes I wonder why they offer this special treatment of 'Ladies First'? According to them, ladies are the "weaker section"???? and can't be kept waiting anywhere so naturally they're given the first preference. Hell! What benefit do we get out of it? Zero! We 'Ladies' are neither amused nor satisfied by these empty words.

From the moment we wake up, we can see the bias. height of the sinks, towel hangers, the shower pods are made with men in mind. All will agree on Bed frames and mattresses that do not provide adequate support for women's hips and lower back, leading to sleep disturbances and pain. Inadequate number of sanitary napkin vending machines or disposal bins in public spaces. Not only sanitation facilities but simple chairs, tables, and switchboards, even if you think of public transport, the design of buses seems to be the most misogynistic. Every other materialistic thing a woman goes through every day is designed for an average male. Women are used to the hardships and adapted to them. Yet few things are left for women's Kitchen Stove! Yes it is designed solely for women!

When a good career opportunity comes in office none says 'ladies first'. When a good training opportunity comes without asking women, men decide 'Oh how she will go leaving behind her family'. Society worship such women who sacrifice their careers for children, who got beaten up but remain married, who bear children after marriage, who only wear traditional dress, who eat after feeding everyone, who do everything for their parents, husband, in-laws, relatives, and society told them. We revere such women. What a pity!

True respect goes beyond superficial gestures and requires understanding and valuing women as individuals. Offer assistance based on the situation, not because someone is a woman. the question is why do women need empowerment to raise their level to compete with men in society?

Like Men ...Women are ALSO living... breathing ...human beings who can be bad, good, stupid, intelligent, selfish, opportunistic, materialistic, smokers, drinkers etc. Instead of focusing all of our efforts on gender equality, we should enlighten our society to change their views and embrace the fact that women can do anything and acquire anything if they are not hindered by social barriers.

Women are not better than men (well, sometimes they are). Women deserve more respect than they currently get, but not more respect than men: just precisely the same amount of respect men get.

Women are as human as men!

We all have something to bring to the table.

No one in the world is equal to anyone, but everyone has an equal amount of talent in different fields.

Men are not better than women, and women are not better than men. The problem with lumping in men and women together is that it ignores individual qualities. Individually, we all deserve to be treated with respect. For example, men have rights even though unlike women they cannot give birth. Not all women who want to will become police officers or pilots and not only air hostesses. Similarly, relationships are based on being equal partners, not on "the husband being the head of the household."

Yes... agree...attitudes have changed considerably over the past 20 years. Traditional gender roles are being challenged, with women making strides in education, careers, and leadership positions.

However, gender inequality still exists, and pay gaps and discrimination persist. Still in most of countries, when it comes to the workplace, there is an even stronger sense among the public that the playing field is uneven. Men earn more money than women for doing the same job, and nearly half say there's a gender gap in hiring and promotions when it comes to the top jobs in business and government.

As per PEW Research, The perception among women that men receive more favourable treatment cuts across generations. Roughly equal shares of Millennial women (51%), Gen X women (55%), Boomer women (54%), and Silent generation women (58%) say that society generally favors men over women.

Patriarchy manifests in various ways across different societies and cultures. These structures are deeply ingrained in cultural norms, laws, and institutions. Many people are unaware of the extent of gender inequality and its negative impact on women's lives. We need to actively identify and challenge harmful stereotypes and biases about women, both individually and collectively.

Should men and women have equal access and opportunity to participate in society? Yes!

Should men and women have equal access and opportunity to participate in the political process? Yes!

Should men and women have equal access and opportunity to participate in the economic system? Obviously Yes!

Should men and women have equal access and opportunity to provide better care for their children? Yes!

It is important to change the patriarchal mindset - of *valuing a guy's 'job' more than a woman's 'job'. Both are equally WORTHY in their own right.*

If a woman is more capable of taking care of the baby does not mean that she should sit in the house. Or a man should not be discouraged from pursuing singing or arts or even as a house husband. They should be *free* to pursue whatever, they like. All people have the right to make their own choices and live the life they want—and that applies equally to men and women.

Companies need to dive deeper into their beliefs, norms, practices, and policies to understand how they position women relative to men and how the different positions fuel inequality.

Treating someone the same is different than treating someone equally. We shouldn't treat everyone the same. All human behaviour, positive and negative, is *human. Men and women included.*

Women's choices should be respected as men. Nothing less, nothing more.

Different yet equal

What could be the purpose of one's life, whether a man or a woman?

It varies from person to person as everybody has different choices, talents, passions, and aspirations.

Like all individuals, they have unique purposes in life, based on their personalities, interests, and circumstances.... some commonalities can be observed among women globally. These commonalities often stem from shared experiences, biological factors, and societal roles.

Women often prioritize emotional connections and relationships in their lives, whether it be with family, friends, or romantic partners. Many women are drawn to roles that involve caring for others, such as motherhood, teaching, or healthcare. This is often rooted in their biological capacity to give birth and breastfeed, as well as societal expectations of women to be caregivers. Inst it?

Women are often known for their empathetic and compassionate nature, which can lead to a purpose in life centered around helping others, advocating for social causes, or working in fields such as counselling or social work. And mainly... Balancing multiple roles! Many women juggle various responsibilities, such as career, family, and community involvement.

Equality does not mean sameness, but rather the fair and just treatment of all individuals regardless of their gender.

When talking about equality, what is being referred to is equal opportunities and equal treatment about matters that are not biological. They just need to be equal under the law, which is to say the rules by which we live.

So, In final words - men & women are different.

They have specialized roles & specific/unique talent sets. But this *difference* does not make them unequal.

They are ***different yet equal. They are a complementary team.***

Who's happier, men or women?

Yeah...it's complicated!

Research studies on happiness and gender have shown mixed results. Also, the discrepancies may be due to the different methodologies used in the studies or the specific populations being analyzed. So we can say Happiness is different for women and men.

But but but...... unfortunately, research shows that women are twice as likely to experience depression compared with men. Gender differences in depression are well established.

Women's hormonal fluctuations, such as those experienced during menstruation, pregnancy, and menopause, can affect mood and contribute to depressive symptoms.

Some studies suggest women report experiencing emotions, both positive and negative, with greater intensity than men. Societies often socialize women to be more open about their emotions, leading them to express and report them more readily.

Men, on the other hand, may be encouraged to suppress emotions, leading to under-reporting. Men might be socialized to hide their vulnerabilities and emotional struggles, leading to an appearance of happiness even when they are facing difficulties.

In many cultures, traditional masculinity is associated with traits like strength and independence. Or.. Achieving success in their careers or providing for their loved ones might make men feel a sense of accomplishment, adding to their happiness.

Men/women might have different communication styles when expressing emotions. Research also shows women are more likely to try and get help and access treatment – allowing them to recover sooner.

Indeed... Happiness is subjective and influenced by a wide range of personal factors. Many women find fulfilment and joy despite societal challenges. But study says Women are statistically more likely to experience certain mental health conditions like depression and anxiety, which can be exacerbated by societal pressures. Traditional gender roles and expectations can put undue pressure on women. The struggle to balance work, family, and societal ideals can create significant stress and feelings of inadequacy. Fair skin, big eyes, a perfect jawline, sharp nose, pouty lips, a slim figure, and whatnot. Setting body and beauty standards is highly encouraged in our society. It's important to remember that achieving a certain standardized "look" does not guarantee happiness or self-worth.

Let's not forget true beauty lies in embracing diversity and celebrating ourselves beyond societal expectations.

Facing the First Foothills

Conquering Self-Doubt

You are not your body weight. you are far more than just a number on a scale.

“Hey...you look like a skeleton”

"Stick figure"

"Too skinny,"

"Will the wind blow you away?"

“Men only like women who have something they can grab onto”

“Curvier girls are so much more attractive.”

“Don't your parents ever feed you?”

“I’m not going to hug you because I'm scared that I may break you.”

Yes ...I grew up with all above... Along with everything said above, I was also referred to as "malnourished" by someone—my own people, I guess! To me, hanger, ostrich, and flamingo were the standard taunts. I have always been extremely skinny growing up and I can't count how many times I've had people tell me that I should simply grab an air because I'm too thin. Well it’s not just random people but some from my own family used to constantly remind me I was too skinny. I may have been underweight, but I was healthy and doing just great. These remarks, and comments might come across as informal/casual, but they serve as a continual reminder of the time that my closest friends and relatives ridiculed me for my appearance at a family get-together.

I ate like any average person, I rarely, if ever, passed on meals and I ate junk food just like everyone else, but I was still told to eat more n more. People were pressuring me to have more, before and even after I got married, to the point that I felt ill and bloated. Being fat was a sign that a person was wealthy and had access to food, while thinness represented poverty.

As a kid, I never thought much of this because like most little kids I wasn't aware of body image and I didn't care. But as I grew up it became so much more prominent in my life.. eventually I stopped liking my body because every single time someone would throw in comments about it, I would think about it later and it would go on and on and on in my head.

A large percentage of underweight people are underweight because they are naturally like that while a smaller percentage try to starve themselves to be underweight.

Both skinny and fat shaming exist, but the reasons behind them are often very different. Fat-shamed people perceive skinny shaming as a "compliment" to the victim. Body shaming is the act of saying something negative about a person's body, the act of making negative unsolicited comments about a person's physical appearance, often implying how certain bodies are better than others. 47% of girls in 5th-12th grade reported wanting to lose weight because of magazine pictures and now "The Social Media'

I remember one of my friends telling me how her friends, relatives, and even strangers regularly commented on her dark skin. "Who will marry such a dark girl?" was a popular running conversation topic at family gatherings. Another girl at school, boys would make fun of her for 'having a Mustache'. There was a girl used to play Tennis at college-level. As a sportswoman, she preferred wearing comfortable clothes that allowed her to play her best game. This often led to unsolicited advice from friends, asking her to wear 'more feminine clothes' to hide her 'thunder thighs'.

The old-school gender dynamics are still at play when men's worth is evaluated upon their success and achievement, and women are on their beauty and appearance as if we haven't progressed very far from the days of dowries when wives were literally sold to their husbands.

Women of all ages can be subjected to body shaming based on their age, such as, "You're too old to have a great body" or "You're too young to have that body." Women going through menopause can be shamed for changes in their body, such as weight gain or wrinkles...

Factors such as cultural norms, societal expectations, peer pressure, exposure to Hollywood and Bollywood, Media Ideals, and lack of awareness around body positivity can make individuals who don't "fit in" more susceptible to criticism. Additionally, rigid gender roles and stereotypes can contribute to the pressure girls face to meet beauty standards because we tend to experience a heightened scrutiny of our appearance compared to boys.

Body shaming, no matter who it's targeting, is important and is a huge issue in the world that needs to be addressed.

It can tear down and break people, it can shatter self-esteem, and it can make living extremely difficult. The size of your body does NOT define your worth. The shape of your body does not make you any more or less of a person. You have beauty because you are a human being who has a strong and courageous body, worth more than what society tries to tell you.

"You're not beautiful because you're better, you're beautiful because *you're* you."

An Inspiring Tale of Tara

Let's dive into the inspiring story of Tara and extract some valuable lessons in a fun, engaging manner.

There once lived a girl named Tara in a charming little hamlet set in the foothills of a magnificent mountain range. She had a delicate structure of body that made her vulnerable to the harsh words of those who didn't understand the importance of embracing one's uniqueness. This lack of empathy led to Tara being body-shamed by some of her peers, a cruelty that weighed heavily on her young heart.

But Tara's struggles weren't limited to her reflection. Tara, her mother, and her grandmother each faced their own unique struggles. Tara's mother had been a victim of Sexual Abuse, which left her with emotional scars that would affect her entire life. She had to face life's challenges alone after her traumatic experience. This dark chapter in her past made it difficult for her to trust others and created a barrier between her and her daughter. They also faced lack of support from the men in their lives.

Tara's grandmother was left alone when her husband abandoned her due to an extramarital affair! This abandonment added another layer of hardship to her life, as she had to raise her daughter and later, her granddaughter, Tara, growing up aware of her mother's painful past, learned to be sensitive and empathetic towards her struggles. That all was not enough that her family struggled to make ends meet. It was challenging for them to access basic necessities and opportunities. Education, a distant dream for many, felt impossibly far for Tara.

The cruel words of others had left Tara feeling insecure and self-conscious about her appearance. This led to her spending most of her time indoors, away from the judgmental eyes of her peers. Her only source of moral support came from her grandmother.

The whispers of self-doubt grew louder, echoing the taunts hurled her way...Would she ever be enough? Would she ever escape the clutches of poverty and ignorance?

But.....Tara had a Dream!

Tara wanted to become Doctor. Grandmother encouraged her to pursue her dream despite the adversity they faced. Every day, Tara would venture to the foothill of the mountain close to her house. Grandmother understood that climbing up the mountain was not just a physical feat, but a representation of Tara's inner strength and willpower to rise above the hardships she faced. The mountain represented the challenges she faced, both internal and external, and climbing it would symbolize her strength and perseverance.

The grandmother shared her story with Tara, recounting the time when she was a young woman, full of dreams and aspirations. She had faced her own set of challenges, but it was the climb that had given her the confidence to face life's hardships. Tara listened to her grandmother's story, she realized that the mountain had a deeper significance in their lives. It was more than just a symbol of the challenges they faced; it was a source of strength and confidence that had been passed down through generations. The grandmother's last wish for Tara to climb the mountain was not only a tribute to her own journey but also a way to instil the same confidence and determination in her granddaughter. Tara felt a sense of responsibility and a strong desire to fulfil her grandmother's wish. She was determined to climb it, as she believed that conquering the mountain would be a metaphor for overcoming the various obstacles in her life.

As Tara trained and prepared for the ascent, her mother supported her every step of the way. With the support of her family and the memory of her grandmother's story guiding her, Tara embarked on her quest to climb the mountain. She knew that this climb would not only help her overcome her own struggles but also honour the legacy of her grandmother and the resilience of their family. As she faced the challenges along the way, Tara drew on the strength of her loved ones and the lessons she had learned from their shared experiences.

Every step she took was met with obstacles - steep inclines, slippery rocks, and unpredictable weather. But the girl was determined. She refused to let these challenges stand in her way. She remembered the words of her own grandmother, who had faced countless struggles in her life and always emerged stronger. She remembered her grandmother's advice to take breaks and drink plenty of water, and she pushed on. 'Keep going, my dear,' her grandmother would say, 'the view from the top will be worth it.' And so the girl persevered, taking one step at a time, never losing sight of her goal. As she climbed higher, the weather suddenly changed and a thick fog surrounded her. Tara couldn't see the path ahead and she started to panic. But then she remembered her grandmother's advice to always trust her instincts and stay calm. She closed her eyes and focused on her breathing until the fog cleared, revealing a stunning view of the valley below. As she reached the peak she also gained a deeper understanding of the metaphor that her journey represented.

With the sun setting on the horizon, Tara began her descent back down the mountain. She couldn't wait to share her incredible adventure with her grandmother and thank her for her wise words. From that day on, Tara never forgot the lessons she learned on her journey and she always treasured her grandmother's advice.

'Sometimes, the most difficult paths lead to the greatest rewards.'

Years passed, and Tara's determination and hard work paid off. She successfully moved out to pursue her higher education, leaving the foothills behind but never forgetting the lessons she had learned there. With her sights set on becoming a doctor, Tara faced the challenges of college life with the same tenacity that had helped her conquer the mountain.

Tara's dedication and hard work eventually led her to achieve her dream of becoming a psychiatrist. Tara stayed back in town. She realized that her own struggles, though significant, were but a fraction of the challenges faced by many. Tara's newfound perspective fuelled her determination to make a difference.

Chapter 2.

The Climb

Step By Step Guide

Step1: Identify Inner Mountain

Tara’s journey was marked by a combination of both internal and external mountains, or conflicts, that she had to overcome. In the story, 'Tara's Journey to Self-Discovery,' the protagonist, Tara, embarks on a journey that leads her to discover her true self. Throughout her journey, she encounters various challenges and learns valuable lessons that shape her into a stronger and more confident individual.

Self-Doubt:

Tara often questioned her abilities and whether she was capable of achieving her dreams. This internal conflict was a constant companion during her academic life and even after becoming a doctor.

Tara is a shy and insecure girl who constantly seeks validation from others. However, as she travels through different places and meets new people, she starts to reflect on her actions, thoughts, and emotions. This introspection allows her to identify her strengths and weaknesses, leading her to gain a better understanding of herself.

Grief and Loss:

Tara had to cope with the loss of her grandmother, who had been a significant influence on her life. This emotional struggle tested her resilience and strength.

Gender Roles:

Tara’s Grandmother also had Internal Mountains like Traditional. Tara's grandmother lived in a time when women were expected to adhere strictly to traditional gender roles. The same is true for her mother. In addition, they both carried the weight of obligations, remorse, and financial struggles as well as maternal worries.

Power of Perseverance:

Tara faces numerous obstacles and setbacks, but she never gives up. She learns to push through difficult times and keep moving forward, even when the path seems uncertain. This determination and resilience ultimately lead her to overcome her fears and achieve her goals. Through her experiences, Tara realizes that success is not achieved overnight, but through hard work and persistence.

Other women, like you and me, have our own inner mountains, just like Tara and the other women in her life. Women often face the challenge of balancing their professional and personal lives. Mostly, women feel their choices are limited or influenced by external factors. Women are often subjected to various societal expectations and pressures. Women face diverse challenges unique to their individual circumstances, backgrounds, and identities. Although overcoming internal mountains of conflicts is a personal journey that requires self-awareness, and patience.

Women may face internal conflicts when striving for financial independence, particularly in societies where women are not encouraged to pursue careers or financial stability on their own terms. This internal conflict can arise from the pressure to excel in their careers while also fulfilling their responsibilities as caregivers, partners, and parents.

Not every woman faces the same challenges or desires the same outcomes. We come from various backgrounds, cultures, ethnicities, socioeconomic statuses, and life experiences. These factors all significantly influence the challenges we face and the outcomes we desire. We have the capacity to make choices, challenge norms, and define our own path.

Imposing a single definition of "success" ignores these individual strengths and risks driving people down unfulfilling paths. Celebrate individual journeys and avoid universalizing one specific path to success. Overemphasizing one path discourages exploration and personal discovery.

Take some time to assess your feelings and emotions.

- Are you feeling overwhelmed, anxious, or uncertain about a particular aspect of your life?

- What conflicts hold you back? Is it discrimination, societal expectations, personal limitations, or a combination? Be honest and specific.

- Think about the areas in your life where you may be struggling or experiencing conflict. This could be related to your personal life, relationships, career, or self-image.

- Where does it stem from? Is it systemic, cultural, interpersonal, or internal? Understanding the root can guide your approach.

Emotions are strongly linked to memory and experience. If something bad has previously happened to you, your emotional response to the same stimulus is likely to be strong. Observe your thoughts and beliefs that contribute to the conflict. Are they based on facts or assumptions? Are they aligned with your values and goals?

Our emotional responses don't necessarily have much to do with the current situation, or to reason, but you can overcome them with reason and by being aware of your reactions. Identify the root causes and explore how they impact your life. At the same time as being aware of your own feelings, you also need to be aware of those of others. When we demonstrate empathy, we show that we care about how others feel, which builds trust and strengthens relationships.

Also consider what results in positive emotions and what is more negative. Remember, you can change how you feel.

Anybody can become angry –

that is easy,

but to be angry with the right person

and

to the right degree

and

at the right time

and

for the right purpose,

and

in the right way –

that is not within everybody's power

and

is not easy.

- Aristotle

Step 2: Understand the Mountain

Know your worth

Understanding your worth and valuing yourself as a woman can have a profound impact on your life. I can say this because I have seen firsthand the change that takes place when you decide what you truly deserve and are willing to accept, instead of letting the wrong people into your life and failing to see your own worth. I'm finally able to tell you to think, speak, and behave as though you are aware of your value. Give yourself some time to recognize and value your good traits. When you value yourself, others will recognize it and treat you accordingly. By setting boundaries and making choices that honour your worth, you send a clear message that you deserve respect and love.

Stress is a normal and unavoidable part of life—but too much stress can affect your emotional and physical wellbeing.

Experts say that almost all of us benefit from social and emotional support. Emotional allows us to feel understood, cared for, and valued, which can significantly boost our self-esteem and resilience. Social support strengthens our social connection and combats feelings of isolation.

Self-reflection:

- **Internal strengths**: Consider what matters most to you in life. What principles guide your actions and decisions? Connecting your strengths to your values creates a sense of purpose and direction. What skills, talents, and knowledge do you possess? Identify transferable skills and untapped potential.

Utilize the wealth of information available on the internet, including articles, blogs, podcasts, and videos related to your specific challenges. Online forums can also provide a platform for connecting with others who share your experiences. Explore online quizzes or personality tests designed to identify strengths. While not foolproof, these tools can provide starting points for further reflection. Strengths come in many forms: They're not limited to traditional skills or talents.

Most Importantly, Don't be discouraged if you don't have all the answers at once. Embrace the journey of continuous learning and self-exploration.

WHY ME?

It is natural for women to sometimes feel overwhelmed and ask themselves, "Why me?"

Lets see some examples, which you can relate to.

At School/College:

Sarah, a college student, is struggling to maintain a balance between her studies, extracurricular activities, and social life. She feels overwhelmed by the constant pressure to excel academically and fears that she might not be able to handle the workload.

In this situation, Sarah might ask herself, "Why me? Why am I struggling so much while others seem to handle everything effortlessly?"

At Marriage:

After getting married, Afreen faces challenges in adjusting to her new family and balancing her career and home life. She feels overwhelmed by the expectations placed on her as a wife, daughter-in-law, and professional.

Afreen questions her decisions, wondering, "Why me? Why did I have to face these challenges alone?"

@Delivery:

During her pregnancy, Katrina experiences severe morning sickness, which makes her question her ability to handle the physical and emotional demands of childbirth. She wonders, "Why me? Why am I going through this when other pregnant women seem to have an easier time?"

@Breakup:

After breaking up with her long-term boyfriend, Rina feels heartbroken and betrayed. She questions her worth and wonders, "Why me? Why did he choose to end our relationship when I thought we had something special?"

@Mother:

As a mother of two young children, Ayesha feels constantly exhausted and overwhelmed by the demands of her children. She questions her abilities as a parent, thinking, "Why me? I'm not doing a good enough?"

@Left-Out Wife:

Lily feels neglected by her husband, who seems more interested in his work and hobbies than spending time with her. She wonders, "Why me? Why am I not important enough to my own husband?"

@Mother-in-Law:

Victoria, a mother-in-law, struggles to connect with her daughter-in-law, who seems to always find fault in her actions. She questions her role, thinking, "Why me? Why am I not accepted by my own son's wife?"

@Daughter-in-Law:

Example: Sandra, a new daughter-in-law, faces challenges in adjusting to her new family and feels judged by her in-laws. She wonders, "Why me? Why did I have to marry into a family where I don't feel accepted?"

There's another problem!

Smart Woman Problem

It took me a while to realize that, in many cases, smart women are disliked by others. Are you afraid of being judged for being smart? Yes ..women do... So if we've made such strides over the centuries with women's rights and breaking so many barriers and glass ceilings, why is it so difficult for smart women to own the fact that they're smart? And even if you do acknowledge your intelligence, why does that still not preclude you from dealing with other problems like people's distaste for smart women in many situations? Why is it often seen as a threat when a smart woman just naturally shows how smart she is?

This gender divide has led to a situation where a smart woman may be perceived as a threat to the status quo or to male dominance in certain domains. Masculinity is often taught and maintained as a status that is superior to femininity. Men have been expected to be the primary breadwinners and decision-makers in a relationship or society. men have been expected to be the primary breadwinners and decision-makers in a relationship or society. Some individuals, particularly men, may feel threatened by the intelligence of women. They might perceive intelligent women as a competition or a challenge to their own self-esteem.

Its not only men but 'some' women consider another woman as a threat /competition for resources, recognition, or opportunities, particularly in male-dominated fields or environments. This competition can lead to feelings of insecurity, jealousy, or fear of being overshadowed.

Intelligent women might have a more direct communication style, which can be perceived as aggressive or confrontational by others. People, especially men, might prefer a more passive or submissive communication style, as it aligns with traditional gender roles and makes them feel more comfortable. I, myself ,have experienced this lot of times.

Some individuals might fear the idea of women being equal to men in all aspects, including intelligence. This fear can manifest as a dislike for intelligent women, as it serves as a way to maintain the existing power dynamics between genders. E.g In a group discussion, when a man speaks about a topic and an intelligent woman challenges his perspective, it is possible that the man might feel uncomfortable or defensive.

The man might perceive the intelligent woman's challenge as a threat to his own knowledge, beliefs, or authority within the group. Human beings often tend to protect their egos, especially when they feel their knowledge or expertise is being questioned. In this situation, the man might feel that his ego is threatened by the intelligent woman's challenge, leading to negative emotions.

People often seek confirmation of their own beliefs and ideas. When an intelligent woman challenges a man's perspective, it may cause cognitive dissonance, as it contradicts his existing beliefs. This can lead to disliking the woman's intelligence as it challenges his comfort zone. Women are often socialized to be more empathetic listeners and nurturers. When an intelligent woman steps out of this expected role and engages in a debate, it can be perceived as challenging the social norms, leading to disapproval from some members of the group.

Encouraging open-mindedness, empathy, and respect for different perspectives can help individuals, including the man in this example, to appreciate and value the intelligence of others, especially women, in group discussions.

We can always encourage group members to put themselves in others' shoes and consider how their actions and reactions might affect others. This can help individuals develop a greater understanding of different perspectives and reduce feelings of defensiveness or resentment. If the man in question is struggling with these situations, offer support and guidance to help him navigate group discussions more effectively. *But Men are always Men and so the women!*

Change takes time, and in above case its good to remain patient, understanding, and committed to fostering a positive atmosphere for discussions. By doing so, we can contribute to creating a more inclusive and supportive environment for everyone involved.

Encouraging and celebrating the achievements of other women can help break down the barriers that have historically limited women's opportunities and contribute to a more collaborative and supportive environment for all.

Women experience various stages in their lives, each with its unique set of challenges and emotions. from the time women are little girls, they're often put into gender boxes. They are encouraged to do certain things and discouraged from doing others because of biological difference.

Additionally, societal expectations and cultural norms can significantly impact how women navigate these stages. Rather than concentrating just on obstacles, it's critical to recognize the advantages and possibilities that come with each stage. Women are remarkably strong, flexible, and resilient throughout their lives, and it is important to honour these attributes.

YOU ARE NOT ALONE

Why did that happen? Was it my fault? Maybe he didn't hear me when I asked him to stop? Was that normal? If it was normal why do I feel scared? All of these questions flooded in mind.....

We all feel lonely occasionally. However, there is a big difference between being alone and experiencing loneliness. That's how I felt too. I have a different perspective on my past experiences now. Adopting a new perspective can help women challenge traditional gender roles and expectations, enabling them to pursue their passions and ambitions without being constrained by societal pressures.

No wonder, post pandemic, the National Alliance on Mental Illness has made "Your Are Not Alone" the theme for 2021. Not all women are saints and not all men are devils but the statistics speak for themselves. One in five women are victims of a sexual offence and one in three women aged 16-59 will experience domestic violence at some point in their lives.

There are so many women walking around with the weight of the experiences they have had following them as they go through life.

Okay, unquestionably it's not your imagination or It isn't just in your head; it is truly happening to you or has happened in the past. We now need to come up with a plan so that nothing that transpired can harm you.. "Why do people reassure others by saying, 'You are not alone?'"

It can mean different things, such as:

"I support you"

"There are people who care about you"

"Others have had/are having the same experience as you"

"I agree with you"

You are not alone in whatever it is that you are going through, whether it be literally, symbolically, or ethically....

Saying that...It doesn't make you feel better.... It doesn't improve your situation.... It doesn't solve your problems ..'

'You are not alone' is not always problem-solving. But it could be a ray of hope for someone. Depending on where you are in the world, there are some gestures that in some cultures are seen as sharing, supporting, giving energy, passing strength, or reassuring the other one. Sometimes just a hug can be peaceful, it's reassuring, it's a kind of "energizer" that passes from one body to the other. Sometimes It's like ...."I may not be able to fix your car that has broken down by the side of the road, but I can sit with you while we wait for the towing vehicle." Your sorrows cannot be shared but knowing someone else succeeded through it helps strengthen your resolve. Everyone experiences loneliness or being left alone once in a while, including you and me.

That also reminds me of a story (real one) told by my friend who was in her 40's. During our long-overdue coffee date, she shared her story with me.

She said, "Even though I'm with my family, I've been feeling lonely lately. I'm not sure why, but I just want to be myself," she stated. I schedule a lot of time for "me time," travel alone, and so on. I was taken aback when this occurred because I occasionally felt alone myself. "Do you think its normal?" I questioned her. She remarked, "At first, I didn't think it was possible, but then I met a lot of like-minded women on social media." I began getting to know them once I joined their group. We formed a club to meet twice every weekend. we share things, we sing, we drink and dance. I gradually began to sense that I'm not alone."

Her idea overwhelmed me.

In the past, I would wonder, "How can someone feel lonely even when surrounded by family and friends?" I then asked the question on Twitter, and my Direct Messages (DMs) were immediately flooded. So many Women expressed recognition of my loneliness. So that again reminded me "YOU ARE NOT ALONE!"

I discovered Nearly a Quarter of the World Feels Lonely when I first started surfing the internet. Americans are currently facing an epidemic of loneliness. More than 9 million people admit to either 'always' or 'often' feeling lonely, according to a recent study – that's more than the entire population of London.

CNN survey, taken across 142 countries, found 24% of people age 15 and older self-reported feeling very or fairly lonely in response to the question, "How lonely do you feel?" The survey also found that the rates of loneliness were highest in young adults, with 27% of young adults ages 19 to 29 reporting feeling very or fairly lonely.

The lowest rates were found in older adults. Only 17% of people age 65 and older reported feeling lonely. Social media is often a tool young adults use to connect with one another, but it can be more harmful than it is good. Feeling lonely can occur at any age, but a recent study found it peaks at two points in people's lives and takes a dive as people get older. Researchers discovered that that people in their 20s had the highest rates of loneliness and another peak occurred in the 40s while people in their 60s had the lowest loneliness levels.

So again I said to myself "You are not alone!"

A recent study published in Social Psychiatry and Psychiatric Epidemiology sheds some light on what makes a person feel lonely. In sum, they suggest that loneliness has to do with the quality of one's relationships as opposed to the number of people in one's life, per se. In other words, many people are feeling terribly alone despite not being alone.

It's a myth to think that having many friends means you aren't lonely.

Not that being alone is always awful. Understanding our existence more deeply can occasionally result from examining our own need for others. It at least encourages us to value and be appreciative of the relationships we already have. Therefore, occasionally overcoming loneliness might be beneficial. Less is more important in determining loneliness than quantity when it comes to high-quality interactions that make us feel important, connected, and capable of valuing others.

People have become less empathetic, more concerned about self–love, care, improvement, image, and help – at the expense of compassion, more controlled and regimented, more standardized, less adventurous, less open to creativity, and less tolerant of ambiguity. Also, we are living in a time where there is an expert for almost anything. We are instructed on how to breathe, poop, make love, what to eat, how to bathe, and what our bodies should look and function like. Others' opinions become truth. We have become so disconnected from our innate instincts and our capacity to pay attention to our bodies and minds that we no longer even recognize ourselves!

Only you can solve your problems.

Neither a hug nor sympathy will solve your problems, certainly not!. Not everyone will be of service to lighten your burdens. Some will sympathize, some will advise, and some will actually help out. But a hug or those kind words, a helping hand can shade the clarity and the energy for you to make decisions, and actions or simply strengthen your inner self.

A lot of people feel hopeless and like they are all alone if they're in this state. Reaching out to others may make some people feel less lost. Let's not forget...a lot of people in the world like feeling that they are connected to others and that if they can overcome it, anyone can. "I feel you" or "It will be okay" or "I'm with you" such kind of words help to remind the person that you love them. It's very calming sometimes.

One can attempt what works best for them.

Sharing your experiences with others can provide valuable insights and help you feel less alone. Having strong social support can actually make you more able to cope with problems on your own, by improving your self-esteem. Emotionally supportive friends and family who see you as capable, for example, and can help you focus on next steps for addressing your concerns.

So turn off your computer, call a friend and ask about their day, look into someone's eyes and smile, tell someone you love them, or ask for help. It's not too late. We humans are social animals. Even though it may appear extremely different for each person, everyone has the innate capacity to connect.

People need to start having difficult conversations and supporting others to share their stories. Read, educate, and inspire others to do the same. Stand for yourself and stand up for others too. Well, If you are encountering someone under stress or any such situation, what least you can do, apart from simply telling them "You are not alone."

First and foremost thing to do is **Listen** actively. You 'should' offer your full attention and empathize with their feelings without any judgment. Allow them to express their thoughts and emotions openly. Most importantly you have to be **patient** and understanding. Remember that overcoming stress takes time, and progress may be slow.

Depending on your relationship , ensure that you also set healthy **boundaries** for yourself. If they don't want to share, let them be.

Don't ever tell them to wrap it up already or stop being a crybaby. even if you don't believe in it ...tell them it'll **all be okay**. Do not make **fun** of their emotions. You can tell them it's okay to cry sometimes. It does feel lighter. You can offer a hug... or offer water to drink or just stay there.

Also, remember it's important to take care of your own **well-being** while helping someone in stress. If you are not able to pacify, you can be guided by professional help.

You have to make an effort.

Often people expect others to reach out to them, and then feel rejected when people don't go out of their way to do so. To get the most out of your social relationships, you have to make an effort.

Luckily, technology makes it easier than ever before to stay connected with loved ones far away. Write an email, send a text message, or make a date for a video chat.

Trust your instincts and prioritize your feelings

Who can be your allies?

Friends, family, mentors, online communities, or professional support systems? Build your network. You don't need a huge network of friends and family to benefit from social support. Surround yourself with positive, supportive individuals who encourage and empower you. On the other hand, distance yourself from those who bring you down or make you feel uncomfortable.

You may not have someone you can confide in about everything—and that's okay. Maybe you have a colleague you can talk to about problems at work and a neighbour who lends an ear when you have difficulties with your kids. Look at different relationships for different kinds of support. But remember to look to people you can trust and count on, to avoid disappointing, negative interactions that can make you feel worse.

Join groups where individuals with similar experiences or challenges come together to share, support, and learn from one another. These can be in-person or online support groups.

Do you enjoy playing tennis, hiking, singing, jewellery-making, or being engaged in local politics?

Select what appeals to you. You're more likely to connect with people who like the things you like. Join a club, sign up for a class, or take on a volunteer position that will allow you to meet others who share your interests. Don't be discouraged if you don't make friends overnight. Try to enjoy the experience as you get to know others over time.

If needed, consult a therapist or counsellor who can help you navigate complex emotional issues and provide guidance in identifying your mountain.

Step 3: Plan Your Climb

Start Small:

Start small and celebrate milestones. A good way to resolve internal issues and accomplish personal progress is to start small and celebrate accomplishments. It enables you to deconstruct your objectives into attainable goals.

Remember: one step at a time

Break down your aspirations into smaller, achievable steps. This will help you feel a sense of accomplishment and progress, making it easier to overcome the conflict.

Assign a reasonable timeframe for each milestone to create a sense of urgency and motivation without causing undue stress. Just like Tara, who utilized her strengths and sought support, it's crucial to assess your own resources. What are your strengths, skills, talents, and knowledge? Who can be your support system? Do you have access to educational resources, mentors, or financial aid? Understanding your assets empowers you to leverage them effectively.

Choose your path:

Even while Tara's narrative can serve as motivation, it's important to keep in mind that each person has an own journey to follow. Selecting yours is not about following someone else's path. However, understanding what led Tara to success can offer valuable insights for guiding your own exploration.

Look beyond conventional expectations and explore various ways to overcome your mountain. Don't be afraid to break traditional moulds. Learn from others who have faced similar challenges, but remember their paths are not blueprints for yours.

Find your tools:

Recognizing strengths, weaknesses, and motivations - Tara identified her passion for medicine and her ability to work hard.

Remember, each "mountain" is unique: Don't try to copy Tara's exact tools. Identify the tools most relevant to your specific challenges and goals. These challenges can be personal, professional, or related to relationships, health, or self-growth. It is essential to recognize that every person's experiences and circumstances are unique, and therefore, the tools and strategies they use to overcome these challenges should be tailored to their specific needs and goals. identifying the most relevant tools for your individual challenges and goals involves self-reflection, understanding your strengths and weaknesses, and being aware of your personal values and priorities.

Once you have identified your challenges, set **SMART goals** for overcoming them. These goals should be specific, measurable, attainable, relevant, and time-bound (**SMART**).

Step 4: Start Climbing

Divide your larger goals into smaller, more manageable tasks. This will make it easier to track your progress

Challenges are inevitable. Learn from them, adjust your approach, and keep moving forward. Ensure you're getting enough sleep, eating well, exercising, and engaging in activities that bring you joy and relaxation.

Action is key: Don't wait for perfection.

Take small, consistent steps.

Setting clear goals and staying focused despite obstacles – Remember how Tara remained committed to becoming a doctor despite societal expectations. Tara actively sought knowledge and embraced new challenges. So remember, the climb won't be smooth sailing. Setbacks and challenges are inevitable. Learn from them, adapt your approach, and most importantly, never give up.

Don't be surprised when things get tough. Acknowledging that obstacles are inevitable aids in your mental readiness and keeps you from being disheartened when they appear. Instead of seeing them as roadblocks, view them as learning opportunities. What can you learn from this hurdle? How can you adjust your approach and become stronger? Tara discovered new methods to overcome physical restrictions and used discrimination as fuel for her determination.

Develop the ability to bounce back and keep moving forward. Don't let setbacks define you. Flexibility allows you to navigate unexpected obstacles. You can lean on your community during tough times.

Draw strength from stories like Tara's and others who have overcome adversity. Let their journeys remind you that persistence and resilience can conquer even the toughest mountains.

Remember, every step you take brings you closer to the top. Believe in yourself, stay committed to your goals, and enjoy the journey as you climb and overcome the challenges in your life.

Chapter 3.

Reaching The Top

Take a View from Top

Tara learns that the journey of self-discovery is an ongoing process. She understands that there is always room for growth and improvement and that it is essential to continue learning and evolving. Through her experiences, she learns to embrace change and view it as an opportunity for personal growth.

It's about acknowledging the sacrifices made, the battles fought, and the lessons learned. Look at the view, for it reflects your incredible journey, a testament to your unwavering spirit.

Understand that the struggles you have gone through have shaped you into the person you are today. Your experiences have made you wiser and more capable of handling life's challenges.

Instead of dwelling on the past, focus on the lessons you have learned and how they can help you grow even stronger. Remember that personal growth is an ongoing process, and every challenge presents an opportunity for learning and self-improvement.

Cherish these experiences as they have shaped your character and equipped you with valuable life lessons. Use your newfound wisdom to guide you in making informed decisions and empowering others to face their own challenges with confidence.

Recognizing new possibilities, appreciating the journey, a understanding the interconnectedness of mountains.

Never underestimate your strength and resilience.

Offer support and guidance to others who may be going through similar struggles. Your experiences can serve as valuable insights and inspiration for those who need it. Support one another, share your wisdom, and create a nurturing environment where women can thrive.

“Stay open to new challenges”

So, fabulous ladies...... let's raise our glasses or Tea/coffee mugs and cheer to stay open to new challenges! Embrace the adventure, conquer the world, and remember – you're stronger than you think!

Celebrate Your Success

Writing down your thoughts, feelings, and experiences can help you track your journey and understand how far you've come. Like Tara, believe in your own ability to overcome obstacles and achieve your dreams.

Every mountain climbed deserves a celebration. Be proud of your achievements, big or small. Remember, you are on your own unique journey, and your success is defined by your own goals and aspirations. You'll realize how far you've come when you look back. You have changed as a person. You have managed every discomfort and challenge with such skill. That's your victory in and of itself.

Remember, progress, not perfection, is the key.

Celebrating small wins is what helps us to achieve the next goal. (Think like a child). Rewarding your beaten self for making every effort to heal and recover by celebrating these tiny victories is crucial to your effective recovery from depression.

Just like any mountain climb, conquering your obstacles is best done one step at a time. Celebrate every milestone, no matter how small. Remember, progress over perfection is key. Tara built her dream brick by brick, studying hard and facing challenges head-on.

Understand that personal growth often involves change, and that's okay. Recognize that you're not the same person you were when you started your journey, and embrace the new person you've become. Your story can also help you gain a new perspective on your journey and the growth you've achieved.

Celebration is personal and specific thing for each of us.

The climb may be long, but the journey towards overcoming conflict and achieving goals is empowering and worthwhile.

Well, while it's easy to buy chocolate or takeout as a celebration for a small win, this is less meaningful and has too many other risks, such as overeating, health risks, and more. Shopping is also not always a great idea as this can lead you to only wanting to do things when there's a monetary reward.

Reward your behaviour (e.g., walking) instead of a result (e.g., weight loss). Behaviour is what you have control over and behaviour is what leads to results.

- ❖ Take time to breathe, close your eyes for five minutes after a strenuous task, or stretch after a difficult work session
- ❖ You can send yourself an email or message congratulating you on actions you have taken.
- ❖ Sit and enjoy your favourite song in your car before work when you make it there on time
- ❖ You can express joy through dancing or playing loud music.
- ❖ You can cook a special dish for you.
- ❖ You can go to a concert or drama or a short trip if that win is big for you.
- ❖ When you celebrate your small wins, sharing them with others doubles the pleasure and happiness. Share it with your loved ones.
- ❖ There is joy in giving, so why not share your wins with others with acts of kindness or charity?

Remember, Introspection is also very important. Sometimes the negative thoughts holding us back go unnoticed by us. Spend some time getting to know who you really are and figuring out what experiences or underlying ideas might be undermining your sense of value.

In the end...recognize that the most important relationship you have is with yourself, and invest time in nurturing and understanding your own needs and aspirations!

You've worked hard,

You've persevered,

and now.....

is the time…

to celebrate.

Success is earned, not given.

Take pride in how far you've come.

Make 'Me' your life partner

There is only one person in your life you are going to spend whole life with ....

that is YOURSELF!

Think about it—everyone else in your life, no matter how close or important they are, will come and go. Friends, partners, family members, colleagues—they are all part of your journey, but the one constant is you. **You are the only person who will walk with you from beginning to end, through every challenge, every triumph, every high and low.**

If you are not okay with yourself then there is a problem otherwise not.

Your 'me' knows you much better than the entire world, and just like a best friend, it stands by you in all weathers. Treat yourself with kindness, patience, and understanding, just as you would treat a close friend who is facing challenges.

The best part about 'me' is that, it works actively when you are miserable, while rests when you are happy. But the problem is that-

1. Either we don't connect with our 'me'.

2. Or we lose connection with our 'me' because of some overwhelming circumstances.

When you achieve something, tell it, it will definitely give a pat on your back and make you feel good about yourself.

Strive to be true to yourself and express your authentic self without fear of judgment or rejection.

Interact with your soul often, keep it alive and active, and make it stronger and influential in your life, this will definitely have some side effects, you may appear a little narcissistic to people, but it will strengthen your identity and never let you feel lonely.

Are you allowing yourself to grow, to learn, and to flourish, or are you holding yourself back? Taking the time to nurture your mind, body, and spirit is not selfish—it's necessary.

Embrace these life-changing tips and watch as your life undergoes a remarkable transformation. Start your journey to self-worth today and create the life you deserve!

Epilogue

The mountain you've just climbed is not the end, but merely the beginning.

As you stand at the summit of your own transformation, take a moment to look around. The view may be different than what you expected. It may be more beautiful, more expansive, or even more challenging than you could have imagined. But what matters is this: **you made it.** You took the steps, one by one, faced the obstacles, and never gave up.

Throughout this journey, you've learned that the mountain is not just a symbol of struggle. It is a symbol of strength, resilience, and personal power. You've discovered the capacity within yourself to rise above your fears, to challenge your limitations, and to live in alignment with your true self.

But the summit is not a place where you stand still. The mountain doesn't stop here. The world you now see before you is filled with possibilities, and the climb will continue—because growth is a lifelong journey. There will be new peaks to conquer, new lessons to learn, and even more inner strength to discover. And that's the beauty of it.

Remember that you are always evolving. Every step you take from here will be built on the strength and wisdom you've gathered along your journey. The challenges ahead will be met with the same courage and determination that brought you to this point. And when the next mountain appears before you, you will know—**you are capable of climbing it.**

As you continue on your path, hold onto the lessons from this journey: that your worth is not defined by others, that your power lies within, and that every step you take toward your truth brings you closer to becoming the woman you are meant to be.

You've already proven to yourself that you can climb your own mountain. Now, go forward with confidence, knowing that there are no limits to what you can achieve.

The journey doesn't end here. It is just beginning.

A Fond Farewell And a Promising Beginning.

Dear Reader,

May this book have left an indelible mark on your heart, reminding you of your strength, resilience, and unyielding spirit. As you turn the final page, take a moment to reflect on how far you've come and the exciting journey that awaits you.
Embrace your unique journey, and always strive to learn, grow, and inspire others.
With gratitude and hope for your continued growth,
Sandy S.
Author

"This mountain is yours to climb,
to prove that no challenge is insurmountable."
Regards
Sandy S

www.ingramcontent.com/pod-product-compliance
Lightning Source LLC
LaVergne TN
LVHW070942160826
845679LV00022B/1886
9798896105190